groovy chick

personal stuff

name .....Megan Thornborough.....

age .....9 years old.....

telephone .....5235 582.....

email .....haven't got one.....

my funkiest friends .....Sarah Holmes + Rachel Briggs.....

my top hobby is .....Badmenton + reading.....

when grow up, i want to be .....Vet. Work animal.....

centre.....

contents

Hi!

Welcome to my second annual. My friends and I have once again collected a whole bunch of cool ideas to keep things groovy for another year! You'll find tons of fab fashion and beauty tips, ideas for your future and fab things to do with your mates. There's a story, puzzles, quizzes, jokes and some super craft projects too. Oh, and if you enter the competition at the back of the annual you could win some cool gear for your next sleepover party!

Loads of love,

groovy chick

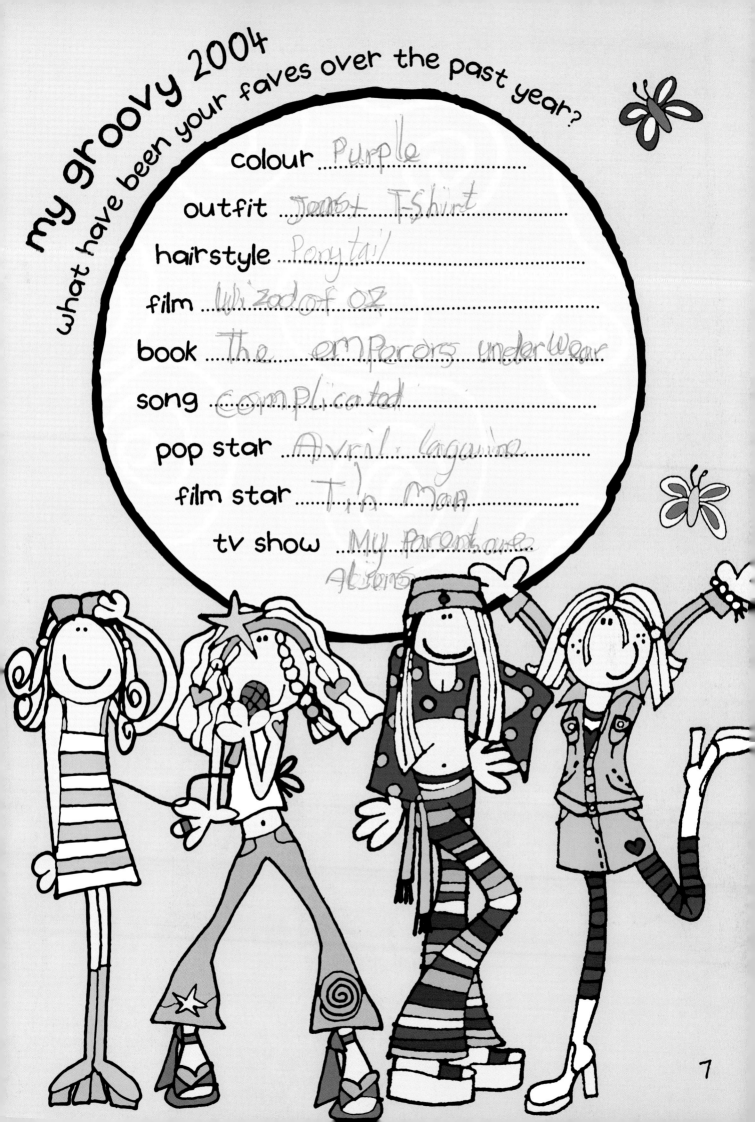

my groovy 2004

what have been your faves over the past year?

colour ......Purple...............................

outfit ......Jeans T-Shirt........................

hairstyle ......Ponytail..........................

film ......Wizard of Oz...........................

book ......The emperors underwear.................

song ......complicated............................

pop star ......Avril Lagavine.....................

film star ......Tin Man...........................

tv show ......My parent are
Aliens

7

groovy chick's latest fashion news

Our girl groovy chick is still the queen of fashion.

Check out her latest tips

for looking super cool.

rainbow chic

Wanna add some cute pastel stripes to your wardrobe? Groovy chick predicts rainbow patterns are gonna explode onto the high street, so be the first in your class to get the look. If you'd rather accessorise, try a gorgeous rainbow bag.

do it in denim

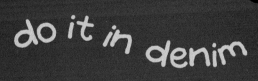

1. A super long denim skirt with a tank top and a chunky belt, finished off with chunky sandals. Cool!

2. A denim mini with knee-high boots and a kickin' t-shirt.

3. Funky denim flares and jacket, plus platform trainers.

top tip
To look taller in flat shoes, dress in one colour or wear something with vertical stripes.

bling bling babe

Try a pastel track suit with a white vest and (clean) trainers, plus loads of bangles, big hoop earrings and chain necklaces. Put hair up in a pony tail or wear a cap.

disco diva

① Choose comfy, stretchy fabrics that let you show off your cool moves.

② Add layers, so when you heat up you can take off a layer and stay cool.

③ Wearing bright colours means you won't get lost in the crowd!

④ Try fun accessories, like sparkly jewellery and hair clips.

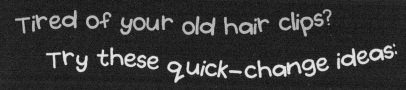

Tired of your old hair clips? Try these quick-change ideas:

★ Coloured hair extensions

★ Glitter hairspray

★ Coloured hair mascara

hair flair

9

pretty in punk

Be a punk princess! Take a rock-chick pink top, add some zips, rips, leather, fishnet tights, a black mini skirt and you've got punk. If you're in to make-up, load on the black eyeliner.

yes, officer

The military look has been around for ages but now it has a glamorous edge. Try satin army pants tucked into heeled boots - pair with a cute vest top or pretty camisole and a camouflage cap to complete your military makeover.

far east funk

Go oriental in a satin kimono top or chinoiserie print dress. Just add a printed silk purse and some red lippy for a touch of far east funk.

what's your fashion passion?

Note your hot tips of the past year, or come up with some new ones.

shop like a stylist
– with hey gorgeous

Top celebs have to look their best at all times. Most of them have a fashion helper called a stylist. Hey gorgeous has collected some cool stylists' tips and tactics for your next mega shopping spree.

1. Wear as little as possible; who wants to peel off and put on a vest, shirt and sweater half a dozen times?!

2. Don't take a handbag; it will only get in the way and you might accidentally leave it in a changing room. Wear something with pockets instead.

3. Get to the shops first thing saturday or sunday morning (better yet, on a weekday morning if you're on a school break). If you go late in the afternoon, a lot of sizes will be on the fitting room reject racks.

4. Check out your fave shops every 3-4 weeks. New stock usually arrives at the beginning of the month.

5. If you can't find your size, ask a sales assistant. There may be more items in the shop storage room.

6. Be in the mood! Shopping when you're in a bad mood won't make you feel better; you'll probably just end up making poor choices.

7. Have a plan. Make a list of exactly what you want before you hit the shops, that way you won't be tempted to impulse buy.

8. Always take a shopping pal for advice.

9. Fill up so you don't flake out. Have a snack so you don't get grumpy and tired with hunger.

10. Take a break. Don't try to find everything all in one go. Take lots of short breaks, have a drink, and compare buys with your mates.

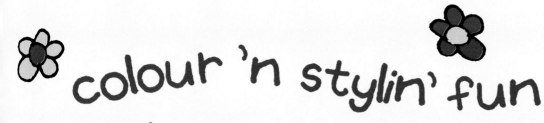

colour 'n stylin' fun

OK, girls, it's time to put your design talents to the test!
Colour in your own funky fabric patterns on the templates of groovy chick and her mates.

you can design your own crazy hair colours too or add some funky patterns.

15

spa day at home

If she's had a tough week at school, groovy chick loves to throw a spa party for her girls!

It's the perfect way to chill out and catch up on all the gossip.

Have a selection of healthy but yummy snacks on hand: tropical fruits like mango and payaya, kiwi and pineapple; flavoured herbal teas and mineral water, fresh fruit juice; salad with tasty dressing; a mix of nuts and raisins. Oh, by the way, a little chocolate wouldn't hurt!

set the scene with...

...plenty of 'chill out' tunes and lots of fashion mags

stretch

yoga

If you're into yoga, do a group class in your living room. Rent a yoga video or get a book from the library to learn a few basic moves. Start with gentle stretching to warm up.

massages

Break into partners and give each other a neck and shoulder massage with scented oil, like coconut or lavender. Rub the oil in your hands before you start on your partner, to warm it up.

mini facials

Wash your face with your favourite cleanser. Apply this simple scrub that's a gentle polish for all skin types:

oatmeal scrub

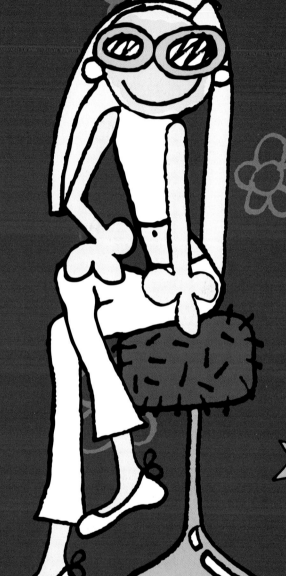

Mix a little cleanser with a sprinkle of porridge oats in the palm of your hand. Gently massage the scrub onto damp skin, then rinse off with cool water. Apply your favourite moisturiser.

manicures

You will need:

- polish in your fave colours
- polish remover
- emery boards
- cotton wool
- small bowls filled with warm soapy water
- moisturising cream
- towels

First, remove any old nail polish. Gently file nails into shape. Groovy chick likes a square style, but hey gorgeous likes her nails more rounded. Try to file in one direction only so you don't weaken the nail. Fill a bowl with soapy water. Soak hands in the bowl for a few minutes. Then try the scrub.

super sugar hand scrub

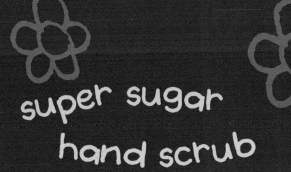

You will need:
- ☆ 1/4 cup sugar
- ☆ 2 tablespoons olive oil
- ★ bowl

Mix the sugar and oil together in the bowl. The scrub should be a thick paste. Massage gently into the hands, then rinse well.

After the scrub, massage a body cream into hands and lower arms. Wipe over the nails to remove excess cream. Polish nails with a base coat. Let nails dry for a few minutes. Apply nail colour and let dry again. For a touch of glam, add a little glitter or costume gem pieces before the polish dries.

18

the private spa

For the ultimate spa on your own, nothing beats a luxurious bubble bath. Turn to page 43 for some fab home-made bubble bath recipes.

other theme party ideas:

fancy dress

chick flick night

dance -a- thon

tropical island

wild west

fashion show

groovy chick's guide to etiquette

Going to a fancy restaurant with the family?

Or how about a formal tea party?

Check out groovy chick's handy tips that are bound to impress!

1. Eat with a fork unless the food is meant to be eaten with fingers. Only babies eat with fingers!

2. Don't stuff your mouth full of food, it looks gross!

3. Chew with your mouth closed. No one wants to see food being chewed up or hear it being chomped. This includes no talking with your mouth full!

4. If there are several courses and lots of cutlery around your plate, start with the utensils on the outside for the first course and work your way in.

5. Always say **thank you** when you're served, and **please** when asking for something.

6. If the meal is not buffet style, wait until everyone is served before eating.

7. Don't gobble. Someone took a long time to prepare the food, so enjoy it slowly. Slowly means waiting about 5 seconds after swallowing before getting in another forkful.

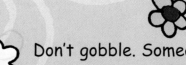
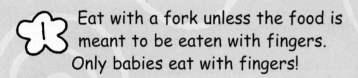
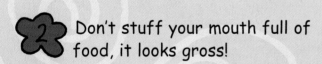

When eating rolls, break off a piece of bread before buttering.

 Don't reach over someone's plate for something, ask for the item to be passed to you.

10 Don't pick anything out of your teeth, yuck! If it bothers you that bad, excuse yourself and go to the ladies' room to sort it out.

11. To wipe your mouth, always use a serviette, which should be on your lap when not in use. Remember, dab your mouth only. Don't wipe your face or blow your nose with a serviette. Excuse yourself and hot foot it to the loo!

21

12 It's OK to put your elbows on the table if you're not actually eating. But, when you are eating, then only rest your forearms on the table.

13 Spaghetti with a spoon? You don't have to. The spoon is there to wind the pasta onto your fork. Twirl the pasta with a fork either by rolling it around in the spoon or just use the fork alone, keeping the fork tip in contact with the plate.

14 Although it's often done in restaurants, applying make up at the table is not groovy etiquette. But, if you do it discreetly, and quickly, then no harm done!

15 When finished dining, place your serviette neatly on the table, to the right side of your plate, not on it! Don't refold the serviette, but don't leave it crumpled up either.

22

tea party tips

1. Since it is a tea party, it's OK to eat with your fingers. But if the food is particularly messy, then use a fork.

2. If all the courses are laid out on the table, eat them in this order: first the scones or muffins; then the tiny sandwiches, and last the sweets.

3. For scones or muffins, break off a bite-size piece, then put a small amount of jam or butter on it.

4. Take bites of the tiny sandwiches. Never stuff the whole thing in your mouth, even though it's small.

5. Don't worry if you do something embarrassing, everyone's there to have fun!

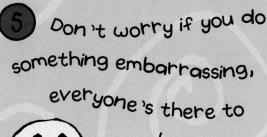

6. If using sugar, be careful to not dip the sugar spoon into the tea.

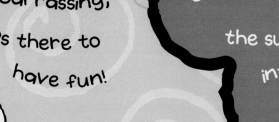

cool careers

hey gorgeous
– make-up artist

roller babe
– doctor

Playing with lip gloss, eye shadows and experimenting with the latest products - what could be more fun than that?! **Hey gorgeous** loves the idea of doing makeovers for a living, on fashion shoots, or for TV and movies. "It's like being a people artist!"

Since **roller babe**'s become mad keen on keeping fit, it's sparked a real interest in how our bodies work. She's fascinated with biology and curing diseases. Time to dust off that science book! "Calling Dr Babe, calling Dr Babe!"

starlet – actress

groovy chick
– fashion designer

Our very own drama queen, could she become anything else but a movie star?! **Starlet** is setting her sights on everything from performing Shakespeare to collecting an Oscar (after **hey gorgeous** has done her makeup, of course).

Groovy chick has a passion for fashion! Sketching designs, sewing and styling from head to toe, she can't wait to start her own fashion business, showing collections in London, Paris, New York. Watch out for the **groovy chick** boutique, coming soon!

24

pop princess - musician

Creating the latest tunes in the pop charts is **pop princess**'s dream. She's already learning to play the guitar (mum and dad wouldn't allow the drums!).

crystal girl - teacher

Crystal girl loves kids, "They're the cutest"! She hopes to be an art teacher, and can't wait to get stuck in with all that paint and clay.

go girl - vet

Go girl's a real animal lover: she'd take in all the stray cats if mum and dad would allow it! Nursing sick Rover and Mitten the kitten is her dream career.

bliss - writer

Day-dreamy **bliss** could spend hours writing stories. She hopes to put all those romantic dreams on paper, to share with the world, if she could only learn how to type with more than two fingers!

other cool ideas

marine biologist
astronaut
interior designer
politician

career quiz

Find out where your current interests might lead you in the grown-up world!

(1) Your teacher asks you to prepare a book report. You can write it, perform a skit, or draw a scene from the story. You:

a) get your classmates to help you perform a skit

b) make a huge artwork with drawings and clippings from magazines

c) spends hours writing and rewriting an essay

d) ask the teacher for guidance, you just can't decide what to do!

(2) Where do you see yourself in 10 years?

a) living somewhere totally different, probably another country

b) taking part in a charity project

c) in college

d) you can't think ahead to next week, let alone 10 years from now!

26

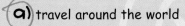

3 If you had a million pounds, what would you do?

a) travel around the world

b) volunteer work

c) invest the money and make it last forever

d) spend it all on friends, family and yourself!

4 What's you fave thing to do on a rainy Sunday?

a) go to the planetarium or a museum

b) go to the cinema with mates

c) do homework or read a book

d) by the time you get up and watch TV, it's almost time for dinner!

5 What's your favourite outfit for a day out?

a) a mix of vintage and a little rock chick, something eye-catching

b) one of your own designs, but nothing too loud

c) a smart skirt and jacket

d) any of the above

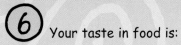
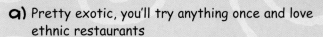

6 Your taste in food is:

a) Pretty exotic, you'll try anything once and love ethnic restaurants

b) Not especially adventurous, and you enjoy cooking your own food

c) Health-conscious, you like eating the right foods and sharing meals with your family

d) You like it all and eat pretty much whatever's in front of you!

healthy food

mostly As
thrill seeker

You have an awesome sense of adventure, and you have lots of get up and go! You'd hate being trapped in an office from 9:00-5:00. A career that never leaves you bored is what you're looking for, something like an astronaut, a police detective, a clothing designer or an actress.

mostly Cs
study queen

Hey there, bookworm! Not only are you smart, but you pour your life into your work and never settle for second best. You can't wait for those years at uni, and see it as the road to your goal of becoming a doctor, a lawyer, a banker or some other high-power position with the workload you crave.

mostly Bs
miss independent

Your independent nature is admirable. You like to do things your way, so they're done right! You like long-term projects and appreciate hard work. A career as a writer, an artist or even the head of your own company might be right up your street.

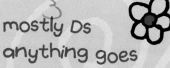

mostly Ds
anything goes

You're young, undecided and have your whole life ahead of you. While some of your mates already have career ideas, you're very open minded and like to take life as it comes.

the secret admirer

It was the day before the big school pop star show and **groovy chick** was in the gym, practising her funky dance routine.

She wasn't on her own for long though. Two boys from her class, **drop dead gorgeous** and **football crazy**, barged in to play some footie of course. They were sooo noisy and distracting **groovy chick** from her routine, but she couldn't really complain – it was their gym too after all. She carried on, wiggling and spinning... then... a football came flying... and nearly hit her!

"Hey, watch it you guys!" said **groovy chick**, "I'm trying to practise my moves for the big show!"

Football crazy ran to get the ball, "Sorry, really sorry," he said, staring at his feet. He was always staring at his feet it seemed. "By the way," he muttered, "Your dance moves are super cool." Then he ran off to have a kick around the park with **drop dead gorgeous**.

Groovy chick always liked football crazy, but he hardly ever chatted to her, and why did he always look at his feet? "Weird," she thought, "I have more important things to do... like get ready for tomorrow night!"

The next evening, at the pop star show, groovy chick and her mates were dead excited. There were five of them in the group: groovy chick, pop princess, starlet, hey gorgeous and roller babe... Ten groups in all were showcasing their talents that night, and the first act was stepping on stage. The lights went out and the music started...

Backstage in a dressing room (well, a little corner in the library), the girls were doing the finishing touches to their hair and makeup. They all looked fab, wearing funky pink mini skirts and tank tops, not to mention plenty of sparkly pink lipgloss. Inside though, the girls were soooo nervous.

"Let's go girls," said Miss Fisher, the show organiser. "It's nearly your turn to go on. You've practised loads, so get on that stage and show them what you've got! Remember, all your friends and families are rooting for you."

Groovy chick and the girls took deep breaths, gave each other a good luck hug,

and made their way to the stage. The curtain went up...

They remembered all the words, sang in tune, and even remembered the dance moves they'd been rehearsing for weeks. When the song came to an end, the girls took a bow, and the audience cheered!

Afterwards, everyone headed backstage to meet their mates and families. The girls were swamped with flowers and cards congratulating them.

"We were fab!" said **pop princess**, "even if I do say so myself!"

"Yeah," said **hey gorgeous**, "we should do this for real when we grow up. I'd love to be a pop star!"

31

When **groovy chick** got to the dressing area, she noticed a small bunch of perfect pink roses. "There's a card," said **pop princess**. "Who's it for, and more importantly, who's it from?"

Groovy chick read out the card: 'Dear groovy chick, you are super cool! Meet me at the park, by the swings, tomorrow at 2pm.'

"Wow, **groovy chick**," yelled **hey gorgeous**, "you have a secret admirer!"

Starlet started planning immediately, "What are you going to wear? We've got a lot of decisions to make by 2:00 tomorrow!"

Groovy chick went home with her family, and all the way little sis **sweetie** teased her about the note. "**Groovy chick** has a boyfriend! **Groovy chick** has a boyfriend!"

When she was finally alone in her bedroom, **groovy chick** read the note again, and again, and again: 'You are super cool'. The words 'super cool' seemed to ring a bell... could it be... Not football crazy?
"But he hardly ever talks to me," she thought.

Groovy chick barely slept a wink that night. The next morning she was up bright and early for the

full home spa treatment: bubble bath, facial, manicure, the works! After much consultation with her mates on the phone, not to mention constant texting, **groovy chick** chose her outfit: a denim mini with knee-high boots and a funky t-shirt.

Hey gorgeous came over to check out the outfit and wish her pal luck with the mystery date: "You look so cool! Text me as soon as you see him. This is soooo exciting!"

Groovy chick set off for the park, but she didn't feel nervous anymore. She was really looking forward to it, her first blind date!

The sun was shining and there were lots of people in the park. She headed for the swings. Lots of kids, lots of parents. Five minutes went by, then ten. No one. Then **groovy chick** saw someone – in a football shirt – it was **drop dead gorgeous**! For a moment, **groovy chick**'s heart sank... just a bit.

"Hi," said **groovy chick**. "Are... are you here... to meet me?"

"Uh, no, I'm not," said **drop dead gorgeous**. "I'm here with my brother."

Groovy chick was so embarrassed she started to run off, without saying a word. She felt her cheeks blushing.

"Hey, groovy chick, wait," called a voice. She stopped and turned, and saw... football crazy, running towards her.

"Sorry I'm late," he said. "My bus broke down and I don't have your number."

What a relief! Football crazy went to get them some ice cream and groovy chick quickly texted hey gorgeous with the news. Then the couple took a long walk in the park, and chatted about all sorts. Football crazy stared at his feet less and less as the afternoon wore on. It was a groovy day, and a groovy first date.

the future looks fab!

Fill in the blanks with your hopes for a fab future.
Check back in a few months – you
may change your mind completely!

When I finish school I'm going to _ _ _ _ _ _

_ _ _ _ _ _ _ _ _ _ _ _ _ _ _ _ _ _ _

and then I'll start an awesome career as a

_ _ _ _ _ _ _ _ _ _ _ _ _ _ _ . I want

to live in an amazing _ _ _ _ _ _ _ _

in _ _ _ _ _ _ _ _ _ _ . Travelling to

_ _ _ _ _ _ _ _ _ _ _ _ _ _ _ _ _

is a dream that just has to come true! I'll take up

some super cool hobbies like _ _ _ _ _ _ _ _ _ _ and

_ _ _ _ _ _ _ _ _ _ . One day I hope to marry the hunky

_ _ _ _ _ _ _ _ _ , and we'll have _ _ _ _ _ _ kids.

I'll definitely stay in touch with my pals _ _ _ _ _

_ _ _ _ _ _ _ _ _ _ _ _ _ _ _ _ _

my best mate will have a great job too, as a _ _ _ _

more than anything, I hope _ _ _ _ _ _ _

34

after-school planner
with go girl

What's your fave thing to do after school?

Hang with your mates?

Choir practice? Footie in the park?

Use go girl's planner to sort

out your weekdays!

monday: ....
....

tuesday: ....
....

wednesday: ....
....

thursday: ....
....

friday: ....
....

35

start a book group
with groovy chick

Book groups are a great excuse to meet up with your mates and get to know classmates better. Oh yeah, and you get to chat about your last good read!

setting up

1. Invite a small group of friends to join. Book groups are a great way to get to know people too. Ask a couple of kids from school who you'd like to get to know better.

② Decide on a time and place to hold your book group. If you start with your house, then maybe your friends would like to take turns hosting at their homes.

③ Once you've chosen your members, send them a note announcing your first meeting.

④ Be prepared to have drinks and yummy snacks on hand! You're bound to get the munchies!

⑤ Have an orientation meeting to:

○ choose your first book (see the tips on page 39).

● set up a group phone or email list. Ask each person to contact the next person on the list when there is book group news.

○ find out if the others would like to take turns hosting and/or leading.

○ decide on regular meeting dates, like the beginning of every month.

⑥ Figure out how you can get multiple copies of your chosen book. Check both school and public libraries.

⑦ Leave time at the end of the meeting to settle on the next selection, and choose the next hostess / leader.

⑧ The only real rules are: read the book and have fun!

37

get chatting

the hostess or leader should...

begin by summarising the story, then describe why she did or didn't like the book

encourage all the others to participate

calm down any heated debates!

book ideas

list your suggestions here:

38

things to talk about

If the chat runs out, discuss

- what was special (or not) about the plot
- which characters you liked or disliked
- what was good, or bad, about the ending

what to read

- ask members to bring a book suggestion to every meeting (gossip mags don't count!), then all the members can vote on the next title for discussion

- if you can't decide on a book to recommend, ask your teacher, librarian or parents for advice; brothers and sisters could help too

write a song - with funky girl

Think you have a flare for music?

Fancy writing a funky new tune? Here are funky

girl's tips to help you write some cool lyrics.

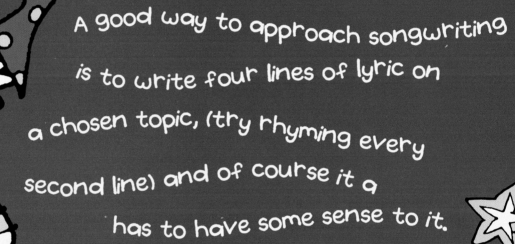

A good way to approach songwriting is to write four lines of lyric on a chosen topic, (try rhyming every second line) and of course it a has to have some sense to it.

theme ideas

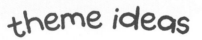

- a good or bad experience/memory
- someone you love, or someone who has had an affect on you
- questions about life
- the future
- your feelings about any of the above, perhaps in the form of a story with a beginning, middle and end

structure your lyrics:

○ write about 12-16 lines of lyric (try to rhyme every second line)

○ divide the lyrics into groups, or verses, of 3 or 4 lines

● choose one of the verses to be the chorus, which will be repeated 2-3 times in the song, between each of the other verses

○ give your song a title; often the chorus concept or hook line, is the one used for the title

what about the music part?

To get a feel for working with music, try rearranging someone else's tune! Choose a favourite song, keep the tune in mind and change some or all of the words; then think about how you might change the music, like quickening the beat, or turning a fast dance number into a romantic ballad.

music or lyrics first?! doesn't matter

Just a thought: if you're not keen on the music part, turn your lyrics into a poem!

creating your own music

Start humming! If you have/play a musical instrument, just let yourself go and play around with different notes. If you don't have any instruments, borrow a cassette recorder from school (if you don't have one at home) and record your hum!

what else can i do?

Choose an instrument and take music lessons!
Join your school choir or music club.
Ask your parents to help you check out community music groups and workshops.

analyse body language

– with funky girl

Did you know that body movements say loads about how people are feeling? Find out what body language says about you and others. You might want to keep these in mind the next time you're talking to someone you fancy!

a bit of a flirt

- ○ Leaning forward and facing you
- ○ Tilting head
- ● Hand-to-face gestures
- ● Lots of smiling
- ○ Moistening lips
- ○ Playing with hair
- ○ Picking fluff off your clothes
- ● Touching you briefly

This person definitely wants to hear more of whatever it is you're saying!

I'm the boss

- ○ Not looking people in the eye
- ● Feet up on a chair or table
- ● Leaning against something
- ○ Moving things around on a table
- ○ Standing or leaning over you
- ● Hands behind head, leaning back

This person feels more comfortable when in control. He or she might have difficulty letting their guard down. You could talk for a bit and see what happens.

friendly gestures

- ○ Open body posture
- ● Smiling
- ○ Repeating glances

These simple gestures could suggest the person wants to get to know you. The best thing to do is to just be warm and friendly right back.

nervous nelly

- ○ Fidgeting, like tugging at clothes or ears, jingling things in pockets
- ● Hands covering mouth
- ○ Sweating
- ● Glances at the nearest door
- ○ Taking a step back
- ○ Crossing arms or legs

These signs show some discomfort. Either the person you're getting these signals from wants to leave, or is just plain nervous. Is he or she trying to keep the chat going (that's a big clue!), and is the person smiling?

groovy-licious bubble bath

Sit back and relax in your own recipe! you can buy most ingredients from your local chemist.

happy apple bath

ingredients:
1/2 cup unscented shampoo or mild baby shampoo
3/4 cup water
1/2 teaspoon salt
1 ounce coconut oil
8 drops apple essential oil

directions

Pour shampoo into a bowl and add water. Stir gently until well mixed. Add salt, and stir until mixture thickens. Add apple and coconut oil and store in a container with a lid. Pour about a tablespoon in warm running bath water.

Apple essential oil is thought to cheer us up when we're feeling low!

luxury lavender bath

ingredients:

4 cups water
1 cup unscented or baby shampoo
3 ounces liquid glycerin
3 drops lavender essential oil

directions

Pour shampoo into a bowl and add water. Gently stir in the glycerin and lavender oil until well mixed. Store in container with a lid, Pour about a tablespoon in warm running bath water.

Lavender essential oil is thought to relax us when we're feeling stressed!

an essential what?

Essential oils have been distilled from herbs, fruits, petals, bark, rind, sap, flowers, roots, seeds, leaves, grasses. There are tons of them and each one has purpose, like relaxing or energising.

Cool container idea: wash out an old jam jar and decorate with your own label.

funky things to make

check out groovy chick's fave projects from the past year!

get in the picture

funky frames   These cute frame ideas make the perfect gift for your pals, and yourself!

the glamour frame
you will need:

★ an old frame, with smooth sides

☆ colourful glass beads or rhinestones, assorted sizes

☆ glue stick

choose a colour scheme and design a pattern for the frame.

carefully glue each bead around frame.

easy peasy!

the rustic frame

you will need:

★ an old frame, with smooth sides

☆ twigs from the garden

☆ glitter (optional)

★ glue stick

Break the twigs to fit each side and carefully glue them around the frame. For a sparkly look, spread a thin layer of glue over the twigs, then sprinkle on the glitter.

cool candles

you will need:

- candles
- beads, assorted colours and sizes
- glitter, assorted colours
- glue stick

glitter

Design a colour scheme and pattern with the beads; you could even make small pictures, like a heart or flower (if the candle is big enough).

Glue the back of each bead and stick to the candle.

Draw a pattern onto the candle withthe glue stick.

Sprinkle glitter over the glue areas and you 're done!

fab flip flops

you will need

● 3 pairs of flip flops
○ small, flat glass beads, in assorted colours
○ super glue

You'll need 3 pairs of flips flops to make 1 pair of platforms. As you need 3 pairs, buy the plain, cheap kind.

○ Remove the toe pieces from 2 pairs so you're left with just the soles.

○ Glue 2 left soles to the bottom of the third left sole, then do the same with the right soles.

● Spread glue all over the centre of the bottom soles, then a thin line near the edge, all the way round.

○ Press the soles together firmly for 3 minutes.

● Glue the beads in a colour pattern around the sides of your new 'heels'.

● Now paint your toenails!

47

luscious lip gloss

For each recipe, mix ingredients together in a small bowl. Let the mixture sit overnight. Transfer your new creation to a small cosmetic pot (available at most chemists), and you're ready to gloss!

vanilla dream
ingredients:
1 tsp cocoa butter
1 tsp coconut oil
1/8 tsp Vitamin E oil
2 drops vanilla extract

sizzling strawberry

ingredients:
1 tsp cocoa butter
1 tsp strawberry essence
1 tsp coconut oil
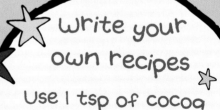

cheeky chocolate almond
ingredients:
1/2 ounce cocoa butter
1/4 teaspoon cocoa powder
1 drop almond oil

Write your own recipes
Use 1 tsp of cocoa butter and a little oil as a base, then add flavouring
Cool!

comedy corner

Get your mates thinking and chuckling with groovy chick's fave riddles!

Q: What do you get when you cross a cat and a parrot?
A: A carrot

Q: How can you go for seven days without sleep and not be tired?
A: Sleep at night!

Q: What do you call a bee born in may?
A: A maybe

what is the quietest building?

a bowling alley, you can hear a pin drop!

Q: Did you hear the story about butter?
A: Forget it, I don't want to spread it around

Q: What's smaller than a fly's mouth?
A: A fly's dinner

Q: What's the best thing to put in a cake?
A: your teeth

brainteasers!

Test your smarts with groovy chick's
brain-teasing puzzles!

letter riddle

Solve each riddle and the yellow boxes will reveal groovy chick's fave creature.

1. I am in book but not in look.
2. I am in butter but not in batter.
3. I am in hat but not in ham.
4. I am in time but not in chime.
5. I am in ten but not in tan.

6. I am in near but not in neat.
7. I am in leaf but not in lead.
8. I am in cold but not in cord.
9. I am in yellow but not in mellow.

write your answer here _ _ _ _ _ _ _ _ _ _ _ _ _

who's that groovy girl?

Match groovy chick and her mates to their outfits.
If you need help, you can find
everyone somewhere in the annual!

write your answers here: a1, b3, c2, d1 _ _ _ _ _ _ _ _ _

groovy things wordsearch

Find all the funky fashion stuff listed below
in the box except for one!
Write the missing word in the space below.
Oh yeah, the words in the box may be written
backwards, forwards, up, down or diagonally!

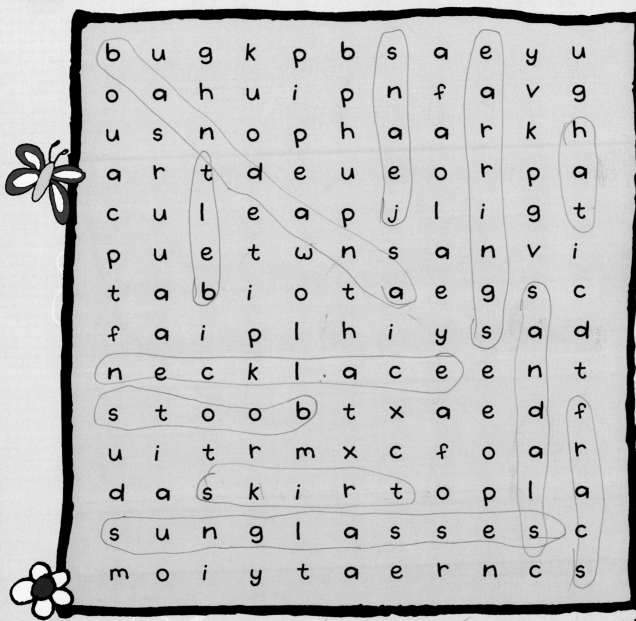

```
b  u  g  k  p  b  s  a  e  y  u
o  a  h  u  i  p  n  f  a  v  g
u  s  n  o  p  h  a  a  r  k  h
a  r  t  d  e  u  e  o  r  p  a
c  u  l  e  a  p  j  l  i  g  t
p  u  e  t  w  n  s  a  n  v  i
t  a  b  i  o  t  a  e  g  s  c
f  a  i  p  l  h  i  y  s  a  d
n  e  c  k  l  a  c  e  e  n  t
s  t  o  o  b  t  x  a  e  d  f
u  i  t  r  m  x  c  f  o  a  r
d  a  s  k  i  r  t  o  p  l  a
s  u  n  g  l  a  s  s  e  s  c
m  o  i  y  t  a  e  r  n  c  s
```

bandana ✓	earrings ✓	jeans ✓	scarf ✓
belt ✓	handbag	necklace ✓	skirt ✓
boots ✓	hat ✓	sandals ✓	sunglasses ✓

the missing word is: _handbag_   53

cool career jumble

Find the answers to the clues in the jumbled letters below.

Cross off each letter as you use it.

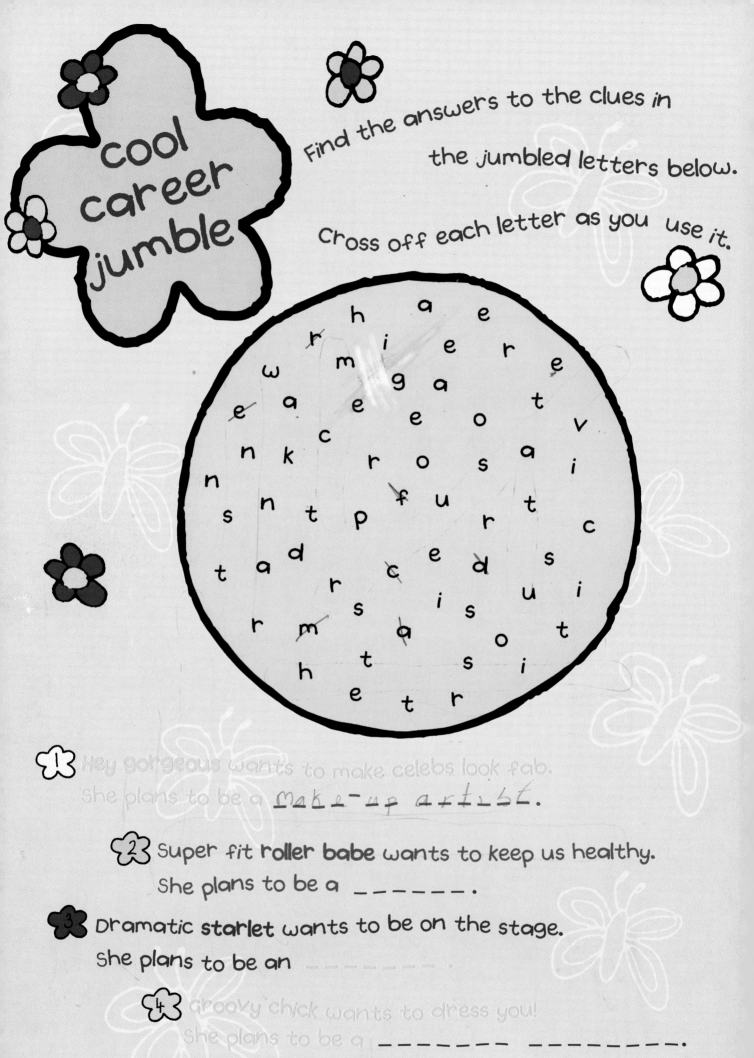

1. Hey gorgeous wants to make celebs look fab.
   She plans to be a make-up artist.

2. Super fit **roller babe** wants to keep us healthy.
   She plans to be a _ _ _ _ _ _ .

3. Dramatic **starlet** wants to be on the stage.
   She plans to be an

4. Groovy chick wants to dress you!
   She plans to be a _ _ _ _ _ _ _ _ _ _ _ _ _ _ _ .

54

Bliss likes to create cool stories. She plans to be a _ _ _ _ _ _ _ _ _ _

 6 Pop princess can't get enough of the latest tunes. She plans to be a _ _ _ _ _ _ _

7 crystal girl would love to work with kids. She plans to be a _ _ _ _ _ _ _ _.

8 ao girl loves animals. she plans to be a _ _ _.

crack the code

 Use the code below to work out groovy

chick's favourite fashion tip.

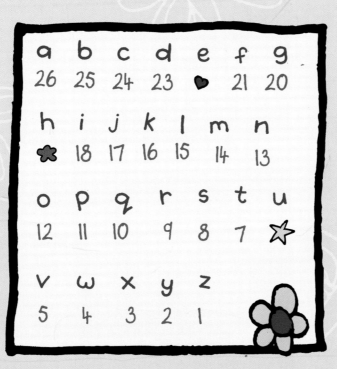

a	b	c	d	e	f	g
26	25	24	23	♥	21	20

h	i	j	k	l	m	n
✿	18	17	16	15	14	13

o	p	q	r	s	t	u
12	11	10	9	8	7	☆

v	w	x	y	z
5	4	3	2	1

7 ✿ 22   9 18 20 ✿ 7   17 ♥ 4 ♥ 15 15 ♥ 9 2

the   right   jewellery

24 26 13   8 14 26 9 7 ♥ 13   ☆ 11

can   smarten   up

26 13 2   12 ☆ 7 21 18 7

any   outfit

solutions are on pages 58 & 59

55

spot the difference

Find 8 differences between these two pictures of **groovy chick** and the gang.

solutions are on pages 58 & 59

year planner 2005

Get organised with groovy chick's handy year planner! Here you can make notes of important dates, things to remember, and all those plans for parties, days out with the girls and other cool things to do!

jan — Katie

feb —

mar — Ke

apr — emily

may — Max

jun —

jul — Laura Sleepover 21st July Rachel + Sarah's coming

aug — Joss Sarah Birthday

sep — Lauren

oct — vicky

nov — Rachel's Birthday

dec —

brainteaser solutions

letter riddle page 51

groovy chick's favourite creature: butterfly

who's that groovy girl? page 52

a. – roller babe matches outfit 4

b. – hey gorgeous matches outfit 2

c. – starlet matches outfit 3

d. – groovy chick matches outfit 1

groovy things wordsearch page 53

the missing word is handbag

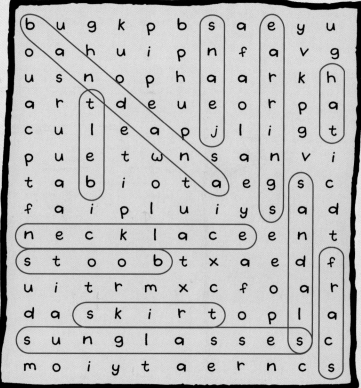

cool career jumble page 54

1. hey gorgeous wants to be a make-up artist
2. roller babe wants to be a doctor
3. starlet wants to be an actress
4. groovy chick wants to be a fashion designer
5. crystal girl wants to be a teacher
6. pop princess wants to be a writer
7. funky girl wants to be a musician
8. go girl wants to be a vet

crack the code page 55

answer: the right jewellery can smarten up any outfit

spot the difference page 56

bang on the door ™ ©

competition

Fancy winning some totally groovy stuff for your next sleepover party?

Simply send us a postcard and the first card chosen in the draw wins.

Here's what you could win:

fleece blanket

monobag

cd player

karaoke machine

how to enter:

1. fill out a postcard with your name, age, address and phone number

2. address the card to:
   groovy chick annual competition
   santoro graphics
   rotunda point
   11 hartfield crescent
   london sw19 3rl

3. stamp and post the card by 1st march 2005

The draw will take place on 15th march 2005.
Winners will be notified in writing by 1st April 2005.

chatter coms

funky recording chatter coms

send secret coded messages

record messages and transmit them to your friends